LYRICAL CREATIVITY
OF
THE
HEART

AUTHOR :
Pro Sawyedul Amin

COPYRIGHT

Book Name : Lyrical Creativity of the Heart

Author Name : Pro Sawyedul Amin

First published by SGSH Publications

Printed in India

ISBN : 978-93-95983-06-8

Price : 250

ACKNOWLEDGEMENT

At First, I am starting with the name **Allah** who created not only us but also the whole universe without whom, we couldn't come in this universe. I am humbly thanking to **Almighty Allah** for giving me the strength to complete it successfully.

I am with elated tears to present those one who love me more than themselves are my most beloved parents without whom I am totally incomplete and the world is nothing for me. A heartfelt gratitude to my most precious parents who brought and raised me into this world and who have gone on to support and encourage me and my creativity without whom I can't stand in front of this stage. I am also extremely thankful them because I was brought from dark to light where I shine and bright as a full moon by knowing what is the value of education. I have been also instructing education since the little age to still now by giving everything without ignorance which I ask and want in my life without whom nothing is possible. They never keep me as a jailer but also give me every opportunity and give up like a freely flying bird. I never feel heartache due to them even their scolding in my whole life. I remember and thank those one until my least breath who feed me everything without taking themselves. Clothes were beautifully wore to me and bathing me by smearing twice a day while I was childhood. My parents are incomparable and totally difference between others.

I have no idea how to thank my dearie grandfather, **Sawyed Alom** however I am giving a hearty thanks to the one who usually suggested me and told to become an well known person in the whole world. He also motivated me if you can not able to be famous, will try to do something which will remain with the name of yours after you will hide from this world. An ambition, to become a renowned engineer is not only mine but also my grandmother. He also warned me if you can not do well anything for other person, don't do to feel heartache due to you in life.

In addition, I am grateful my most adorable siblings, especially my respectable elder brother, **Sawyeddullah** is the one who corroborates me batter than the whole family. He is not only my endearing elder brother but also my special tutor and best friend who indicates me the real ways of life and warns me neither to do nor go on the wrong ways. I was never felt lonely but he always be in my side and friendly keeps me cheer as a friend. If I ask anything from him, he gives me immediately without taking permission from my parents.

I am frankly thanking to my honourable teacher for guiding and teaching me without whom I am nothing. Initially, I could realize which is wrong or true in my life due to them. I have been thought discipline and education, which has the most power even it can change the world. They also made me as a great human and a shining star in my life. Even I can never forget those persons who thought me only a letter in my life.

I am really sending gratitude to my dearest friends who always lend me a hand which I can not ask and mention in front of my family. They always stay with me if I feel either happiness or depression. I was kept on joyful life and support all my activities. They never depend on my pocket either they have or not.

I am frankly thanking to **"SGSH PUBLICATION"** for giving me this opportunity to publish my dream book with their wonderful publication **"Spread Goodness and Spread Happiness"** and helping me throughout the journey of this lyrical book, without whom this book would not have been possible.

Finally, I am thankful every soul who gave me a hand to bring this book to its fruition. I am gratitude to the readers who are reading this wonderful book and wishing good and bright future. Guess every readers probably can gain emotion and sentiment. Hope motivating me to create more amazing things in the life.

ABOUT THE BOOK

LYRICAL CREATIVITY OF THE HEART is **the omnibus of Emotional and Sentimental poems** which not only opens the rhythmic heart but also listens the soul whisper of the bard. Lyrical creativity makes the author to think emotional feeling through the core of heart and soul that occurs either the highest delight or the deepest blue. This enthusiastic florilegium was penned down by the author own various imagination generated from the heart and conscience.

Those one who the more will read this florilegium, the more will experience a roller coaster of extreme emotions. A must try to indulge in the reliable emotion that causes in life as you read. Hope this is perhaps the most superb and essential for you all.

ABOUT THE AUTHOR

Pro Sawyedul Amin, a student of Myanmar and a poet of Rohingya was born early on 3rd, December 2004 at a "golden village", Nga Yent Choung by the Mayyu River in Buthidaung Township, Arkan State, Myanmar. There were forests around the village. His father, **Amin Ullah** was a business man after graduating from the Muslim School, Madarasah and his mother, **Forija** was a housewife after getting married. He was their second child among their children.

His babyhood was an adorable period due to his parents so they gave everything which he needed and wanted to take. His whole childhood was a wonderful time in his life. Every evening he would gather with his childhood friends to play different kind of sports in a wide field near the hospital and down of the police station after returning from the school then they used to bath together with enjoyable in the river. He never felt alone that's why his childhood chum always be with him and made him graciousness.

His classmates were both Muslim and Buddhist as children and teenagers, they studied and learned together freely and regardless of religion or ethnicity at Basic Education High School Taung Bazar. He was awarded a lot of prizes from that school.

He excites to visit with his friends to a new destination. Whenever he travelled with them, he felt comfortable and fresh so one day, he considered that if he travelled all over the world, how much he felt more than his town. He has been planning to travel the whole world since that day when he was at class six.

From a little of age when he was at class seven, He saw that his community was facing different kind of challenge in neighbouring villages so he wanted to help his community so he decided to become a renowned engineer and then began to study hard toward his goal. When he first knew that education is the most powerful tools, he wished to study more and more education at least getting degree from any college or university in his life.

One day, suddenly not only he but also others woke up to hear much voice of guns firing from the police station at 3:00 AM on 25th, August 2017 after that military raided and arrested his community. His friends and his neighbours move into the forest while his family hid inside their home. After six days his family including him began the long journey in the monsoon rains, facing different kind of hardship and genocidal persecution. They needed ten days to arrive near border of Myanmar by walking with their material. Finally, they have fled from their exile into Bangladesh on 11st September 2017 when he was at class eight. Then they began their new life as "Rohingya Refugees" in bangladesh.

Nowadays he lives with his parents, a elder brother, **Sawyeddullah** who is the journalist and leader of entire Rohingya minority and he has built an organisation namely "Rohingya Students Network" (RSN) focused on bringing peace, civic education, awareness of gender-based violence and human rights in the camps and his brother also studies with the major of "BA ELL" at "International Islamic University Chittagong" in Bangladesh. He has four younger brothers and sisters in the world's largest Refugees Camp in Bangladesh, Jamtoli Camp 15, Block D 5, where he has completed class ten and dedicated himself to learn new skills. He has studied and completed many online course but he studies BSc Engineering from online course of University of the People from USA. He tries to do something good for his community. Finally, he started professionally to teach education to the children of his community because they can distinguish which is true or false.

He interests reading books and writing. Once upon a time he penned a story about his life then it has been published as a literature in worldwide so he desired to become a noble poet and a prolific author to help every human as a literature contributor the whole world. In 2020, he started his journey in the world of poetry. Poetry is a part of his life so he began to write different kind of poems. He trusts poetry is beyond powerful. He was awarded different types of prizes and certificates from many International poetry platform. He is the Chief Moderator of "Rohingya Literature Garden". He participated as a co-author in more than hundred anthologies and he has compiled more than twenty anthology. He was awarded many types of awards and perks from different kind Publications House. He has become a Project Head of MV Publications. He also attempts to publish in worldwide his own books. He dreams to back to his motherland one day. He will never forget to go back home even he will die.

Contact With ;

Whatsapp : +8801852342245
Gmail : sawyedulamin158@gmail.com
Instagram : pro_swayedul
Twitter : @sawyedul
Facebook : Pro Sawyedul Amin

INDEX

MY DEAR SWEETHEART

My dearest sweetheart is the oneself
Who never depend on for my own pelf
I will want to hand out everything kindly
Who can sacrifice even soul for me really

The one will be imagined in my peace mind
Whose civilization is very favorable and kind
I will theorize the one in my life as a soulmate
Whose innocence face, a rare smile animate

The one will be loved in my life none stop
By whom is not lovelorn doing me a drop
I will give up a place in my heart forever
By whom is not broken my heart never

The one will be accepted like a special admirer
Whose affection has attraction more than other
I will assume in my life as my darling spouse
Whose aim is not destroyed my real life to use

LOVE AFFAIR

There is a romantic song of my best choice
That is found in your the most appealing voice
Your enchanting face has an endearing smile
My attention deson't change if I see from a mile

Your vivid eyes have a whimsical light
Which you romantically peek me at night
Your sparkling face illuminates as the full moon
If it falls in my vision, my heart can not wait soon

You have two silky lips like roses are sweet and red
I would like to kiss with it however it is feared
Your physical fitness is looking very soft
I wish to speak with you but I afraid oft

Your hairdo is very charming that flies cutely in wind
It makes me to feel cheer and peace in my mind
Your body skin colour is as pretty as deity
You come in my dream when I sleep with self-pity

LOVE MATCH

Love match has different kind dreams
Which is not as like as chocolate creams
It is too easy to do love match with romantic
For which too much like hard work guy and politics

Love match is a romantic relationship doing
Which is based a spontaneous mutual feeling
It deserves and rely on both selves satisfaction
That is materialized because of the emotion

Love match has cloying sentiment with fancifully
Which is not left from love muscle easily and swiftly
There is an intense feeling of affection in love match
That can not be measured and compared to catch

Love match is constructed with much romance forever
That's why love match is not broken in lifetime never
There is an affirmation of the power of love in it
Which has the most aptitude if together stay with fit

ROMANTIC LOVE

Romantic love is gotten due to good luck
Which will be discovered, I will never chuck
Romantic love has both kisses and hugs
Which is remembered, I need to drink drugs

Romantic love makes that I can feel sweet
When I am going to summon you to meet
Romantic love captures pure in heart of mine
When I will fall in confusion to determine

I would like to stay with you in the romantic love
But I have no idea about affection how to prove
I want to establish a place alone in your heart
But I do not know deeply how to take part

I will absolutely crazy for you and break fence
If I will be shown faultlessly your lovely romance
I can be indicated what is romance to be as a tutor
If I were your endearing beau and close suitor

CRAZY FOR LOVE

I am crazy for your affection
If you don't accept my attraction
I fall in love you without imagine
If you ignore the attention of mine

I crazily look for you with lot of way
Where you go for playing day to day
I nonsensical visit toward that place
Where you go to take rest with peace

I pick up an attack without investigation
When you are disturbed any sexual action
For you, I poke his eyes to be blindness
Who looks you with view of badness

I spend my all money to avoid your issue
If you make me to cry and make me to rue
I am ready to sacrifice my soul for your love
If to mingle my life, you totally disapprove

FLOATING IN LOVE

You are loved by me a lot
Because of you are very hot
I impress you are adorable
Due to you are so remarkable

You are selected by me the one
For me, everything you will have done
I can understand you are very kind
So you can take place in my mind

Your mouth sounds is very sweet
When I would like to speak to meet
You are so amazing and marvellous
my darling is you the world famous

Your face bright in my sight
As the moon shine at night
You are floating in love of my
Like the cloud fly under the sky

REAL LOVE

Oh my love! Oh my heart!
You are my body part
My soul cries only for you
Every time, I miss you

Please accept, I love you
I can't survive without you
Because you are my half of life
You are requested to be my wife

You are my half of one
So wish love is done
If you hurt any pain
It is felt in my heart certain

You are an apple of my eyes
Lack you, l will die
You don't come in front of my sight
I see the world be night

You will not mingle in my life
I will suicide my self with knife
With you, I have only love
Oh my dear beloved!

WHAT IS LOVE

Love is not only magic but also blind
For which needs so hard working to find
Love is not only heartache but also tear
Which is very dangerous so have to fear

Love is a kind of fire for the life period
That burns the heart so must be avoid
Love is a big lesson so have to learn
That consumes all money of the earn

It is love that makes the world darkness
When falling in love with cheerfulness
It is love that is more bitter than bitter gourd
When information of dissolution is heard

Much pain is felt by love to see face to face
If the love is the deepest in the existence
A lot of suffering is facing to forget and release
If love is done with much romance and promise

BREAKUP FROM LOVE

I wouldn't like to stay with you both
When it came out from my mouth
I didn't consider like this was a Breakup
I never know there is no turning backup

The last time my lips had a little smile
It was taken from me after while
Inside me, I drowned in tears sea with tension
But nothing was talked to anyone in depression

If I remembered our first kiss
I hoped that I couldn't miss
It made darkness my life of bright
I went anywhere to stand up and fight

I was trying to control my self
My pain was not accented as like as elf
If I revived you, l was very fool
To forget you, l wanted to drink alcohol

But alcohol is injurious for health
Your love destroyed all my wealth
The opening doors of my love was closed
When you left in my life for doing lose

BROKEN HEART

My heart was broken and split however
I was died for your life forever
The windows of my heart was locked
When I was scolded and mocked

My heart excited to look your cute face
Due to It have given me a long space
My broken heart had become a hole
When my love and my heart you stole

You came in my dreams at night
While I remembered your right
All over the world came crashing down
I am standing with a broken heart of own

My heart has turned to solid stone
When you hollow and left alone
My broken heart was the dead of me
It was not simple to see

FEELING ALONE

Without you, it made to feel alone
When in the life you have really gone
The pain of being alone made tired
If you were waited long time with bored

Boredom was felt lonely to stay
If you didn't meet once a day
Because of you felt headache
When suffered from heartache

Score was gained by some one
Whenever lived and worked alone
Much trouble was hardly faced
Wherever living alone was forced

Darkness was felt every day and night
While single life started with the plight
Felt like a orphan was not put an end
While fell danger without lend a hand

CRYING WITH PAIN

We feel so pain without smile
Since we were born in our exile
We have been suffering with fear
So our eyes fill with unending tear

We are as death in our future
If we survive on life of torture
We get misery like grief of hell
Where has unlimited woe if to tell

Without hope, we stay on trouble
So we never inhale with enjoyable
Our hearts are broken with ache
To go on facing much heartache

Whole night we dolefully weep
So we can't comfortably sleep
We were probably born for cry
Due to tear, our eyes never dry

MY TEAR

My tear flew from my two eyes
When you left me to say bye
With my tear became a river
When you forgot me forever

Due to you, dropped much my tears
So I will never presume as my dear
My tear was exhausted and dry
For you, I will never sorrow and cry

The eyes are filled with tears of mine
When I talk about my previous lines
Tears are tried to hide from anyone view
When I would like to feel my mood new

I cry tearfully alone on my bed at night
If there is neither your beauty nor light
I feel very uncomfortable with tear pain
If there is a sound as pattering of the rain

MY DREAM

I saw an wonderful dream the whole night
Which I went a risky place with a gun to fight
I was bravely attacking to foe like an army
If I was alone to clash them at night of gloomy

The more dark was, the more they began to shoot
Neither I try to defeat nor try to accumulate loot
I gained much peril not because of adversary
But because of crossing the densest shrubbery

I devised new way by cutting bushes to get location
Where enemies hid to shoot and fire with protection
The more near I arrived, the more careful I quietly sat
Because I could take position to cover firing bullet

Suddenly a bomb exploded between attacker and me
I woke up after hearing voices of bomb at that time
I have decided to be a soldier of country that day
Unfortunately, I have fled from motherland to away

MY AMBITION

I have some fundamental ambition
Which I did nothing in my past duration
I have been dreaming since my childhood
When everything was distinguished good

My intention is to travel all over the world
Since I tripped with classmates in cold
I tried hardly from early age for journey
But I didn't reach at my aim due to money

My goal is to become a renowned engineer
For which I infinitely wait and rely with cheer
I try to study and learn about engineering
But nothing is possible if I do hard working

One day, I penned an essay about my future
Which has been published as a literature
I had been penning many stories and poems
It has been edited and reviewed from platforms

I wrote poetry and got certificates and trophies
Which has been awarded from many anthologies
One of my ambition is to be an author which fulfilled
When one of my poetry book has been published

FRIENDSHIPS

Friendship is the best relationship
No sorry, no thanks in the friendship
Friendship is not measured by time or length
That gives much strength

Friendship is an enjoy land
No sadness if together hold the hand
Friendship is an wonderful flower
That has a lot of power

Friendship is like a sweet cake
Everybody will not able make
Friendship is a diamond Bangle
Everyone can not mingle

Friendship is a pot of gold
Everybody will not able to hold
Friendship is a happy time
Anyone can not give crime

Friendship is the most important thing
Which is not forgotten about everything
Friendship is a golden life
Between husband and wife

WHAT IS FRIEND

There are many types of friend
Some attempt to give a hand
Some have habits of honour
Some have selfish behaviour

There are many kinds of crony
Some are so droll and funny
Some speak as like as honey
Some rely on other one money

There are many separate mate
Some assume as a soul mate
Some keep in the heart grimy
Some presume as like as enemy

There are differences in friendship
Some mingle as a companionship
Some make the relations is valuable
Some try to decrease respectable

CHILDHOOD PAL

Oh my dear childhood pal
With you, I was playing the football
You were feeding me the food
When I was babyhood

How to walk, you learned me to hold
While I was two years old
How to swim, you taught me in water
When I didn't know better

You were carrying my tool
While I was coming at school
From you, much help was gotten
Which I can not have forgotten

You had not eaten without me anything
If you wanted to eat something
With you,I was doing a lot of funny
Oh my dear childhood crony!

STUDENTS LIFE

Students life is very simple and pure
Where everything can do to make sure
Life of students is very sweet and funny
Where can meet different kind of crony

In students life, should have high thinking
With the best sense of understanding
In students life, should have hard working
With the knowledge and education studying

Time should be respected in the life of students
Which has a lot of advantages and confident
Behaviour should be good in the life of students
For which presumed and civilized like a gent

In the life of students, should be honest
Because in all of the policy, it is the best
In the Life of students, should be helpful
To get from elders blessing with thankful

SCHOOL LIFE

School life is really bliss and delight
Which makes future life is very bright
Learning in the class very nice and well
When teaching with reading and even spell

School life is best moments of life with joys
Where meet every friends include girls and boys
Playing together different kind of sports and run
Where working hard to win the game with fun

In the school life, time spend are unforgettable
Where some of the mistakes are not acceptable
Waiting for the bell to ring is very deeply exciting
If some periods in the school life were so boring

In the school life, attempts are hard without rest
From the admitting day to succeeding final test
If studying is well, no need to worry and face fear
Also absorb more and more benefits for next year

EDUCATION IS THE BEST

Education is the best thing for us
Which is in our lives very precious
The person who has not education
Is equal to the earth lack sun condition

Education is the key to unlock the freedom
Which can defuse from our life boredom
The person who has educated any where
Is equal to birds which can fly everywhere

Education is the movement of our sight
Which can change from darkness to light
Soldiers own the most powerful weapon
Is equal to the person who belong a pen

Education is the passport of future to success
Which is inheritance for generation can possess
An uneducated nation which has developed
Is equal to a hamlet which is undeveloped

ENGLISH IS EVERYWHERE

There are many languages around the world
Which is not like a child's play to count in field
Among them, Five language is very renowned
English is first language of international owned

English language is spoken worldwide
From all languages which were collide
English language is known everywhere
Which is a piece of cake to use any where

Speaking in English is as nice as gold
That language should be used to uphold
Speaking in English can be spoken easily
So do not be fearful to express it freely

English language is as simple as water
However, no need to shy to say another
English language is the most favourable
If attempting hard, nothing is impossible

The MOST SPECIAL TUTOR

You are the most special tutor of our school
We are taught by you the lesson with cool
You keep us on enjoy life in our class
You always try and think for us how to pass

We are indicated a lot of way in our lives
One of them, staying together as like as hives
Where they live together like the shape of sunflower
So the group of bee has a lot of power

We get from you a lot of qualifications
Specially, much interesting education
Which is the most powerful weapon
That can change the whole world soon

We are given much knowledge and advise
Because you would like to see us as wise
Your aspiration is that we will be very famous
You are the one who consider every thing for us

You allow us to do according to our inclination
However, You usually give us many instruction
If you don't come at class, your chair is space
At that time, we can not feel completely peace

ROYAL FAMILY UNITY

Royal family unity has the most powerful
Other one can not make them thoughtful
There are much peaceful in royal family
Every problems can be solved easily

There are much love between each other
So they take and eat everything together
If one of them don't arrive with safe on time
They don't sit and sleep but wait to come

They never give up to feel alone with sad
Also they keep joys when time is going bad
They never fight and scold with one another
Their angry cool down and melt into water

They live and stay home as like as bee hives
They respect and regard each other in lives
They do everything with unity is so precious
So that kind of royal family shall be famous

MY UNIQUE HERO

A person whom l admire very much is my father
He didn't do to get heartache to my grandfather
He gave everything which my grandfather needs
If he took meals, with hand my grandfather feeds

My father gave to my grandmother happiness
With the love affection and truthfulness
There is always a place for him in her body part
Which shall not be broken is known as her heart

My father is the best person like a philosopher
Who gives to my mother a lot of love batter
Every thing without my mother, he never ate
In your life, they both stay as a soulmate

My father is unique hero as like as robot
He shall be assumed the best in my life who I got
He was sacrifice for me everything whenever
That's why, I never obliterate you in my life forever

DEAR FATHER

Oh my dear father
You loved me batter than other
When you gave me a toy
I was a lot of enjoy

You didn't forget to bring me jacket
If you went to market
You bought some biscuits from any shop
When you came back from job

You never warn to do anything
If I wanted to do something
You found me everywhere
If I did not be with you there

You held for me a happy celebrate
In my happy birthday date
You gave me a gift in my first birthday
Which I can not forget still today

MY ADORABLE MOTHER

My adorable mother is very sane and kind
Who can keep cool and fresh my blue mind
My tears were closed in my eyes to be dry
When pain and sickness made me cry

My body was softly sat and watched
When I was sleeping on my cradle bed
I was bath twice a day to keep clearing
During the time of morning and evening

New clothes were beautifully wore to me
If I went to travel anywhere from home
My hair was combed with oil of coconut
While for school with classmate I got out

Walking was taught to hold my hand
When I couldn't move alone to the land
I was fed with hand every meal and food
While I was running the age of babyhood

ELDER BROTHER

Elder brother is the dearest
In every work he is the best
He is the most helpful of parent
So everyone presume as a gent

Money is earned by elder brother
So parent love him more than other
Parent allow to do everything better
So he manages every home matter

He kindly looks his younger brothers
He is supported especially by mother
His younger sister is never little hated
Their needful thing is fully completed

He never consider about his future
He is the one among the all creature
This kind of elder brother is needed
For the whole family is goodly leaded

JEWELLY VILLAGE

Nga Yent Choung is a huge and jewelly village
Where has more than twenty wards for older age
It is probably very wonderful place among Myanmar
Where has a very broad market named Taung Bazaar

There is more than two thousand shops in Taung Bazaar
Where every material is not rare but available even car
There is a High School, BEHS TBZ between mosque and temple
Where education is learned regardless of religion and simple

There is a hospital with the full of specialist doctors
Where every malady is cured well in different sectors
There is a big police station beside the hospital road
Where police force is stable with justice of the peace pad

A cross the village middle, there is a wide Mayyu River
Where much vessel come with loads and people ever
Next to the Taung Bazaar, there is a sandy river shore
Where different types of spots are played more and more

MAYYU RIVER

The river which is very renowned in Rakhine State
It's named "Mayyu River" but forgot naming date
The river is not only very deep but also very wide
Where has river bank and sandy shore both side

Foreigners visit by speedboat for checking office
Driving quickly across the river with noisy voice
People travel from rural to urban area of country
Riding and crossing along the river by boat hurry

Breeze blows towards sandy shore and river bank
Where youths gladly meet friends to stand like rank
There are playground for playing in the sandy shore
Where players play different sports more and more

Fisherman throw and set up different net for fishing
Teenagers compete to cross the river by swimming
Children take bath with friends and play to float
People take a riding to pass river ferry by ferryboat

GOLDEN MYANMAR

Myanmar is a humanitarian and golden country
Where people live and educate without worry
Democracy is filled in Myanmar with ordinance
Where is prevailed by justice and independence

Myanmar is a peaceful country without ail
Where equal rights and correct policies prevail
There are good communication with nationality
Where is no discrimination between ethnicity

Myanmar is delightful and pleasurable location
From where people can absorb fully satisfaction
Myanmar is a safety and fearless place and land
Which is encircled with thorny chains in borderland

Myanmar is a development country in education
Which is too easy to learn without instruction
Prime economy of Myanmar is grain and rice
Which is cheaper than other countries in price

PEACEFUL LIFE

Life of peaceful depends on independence
Which has equal rights and correct justice
Life of peaceful is gained from the parent
If in the whole world, they survive and present

There is peaceful life in health of the best
Which has neither any sickness nor pest
There is peaceful life in truthful friendship
Which has very close and deep relationship

Staying with peaceful life in the mother land
Where has many relatives and childhood friend
Living with peaceful life in rural batter than town
Where has neither murder nor crimes are grown

Peaceful life is absorbed during going to school
If education is studied and learned with cool
Peaceful life based on neither poor nor rich
Because it can't be brought and got to search

LIFE OF ROHINGYA

Rohingya life is full with hardship
Because of there is no leadership
Rohingya life is defective with humanity
Due to there is no unity between community

Much challenge is faced in the tent by Rohingya
Where they live densely together is not mega
Rohingya are encircled with thorny chain like a jail
From where they can not go outside and set sail

They have not under feet land of their own as gold
So there is no value of Rohingya all over the world
There is too admiration to respect between community
So dignity of Rohingya is lower than other ethnicity

There is too high school to study better position
So Rohingya life is destroyed without education
The more ration they eat, the more weak they become
So some of Rohingya struggle and try to go back home.

SITUATION OF THE CAMP

Refugee's camps are as like as jail
Where everyone's ambition come fail
Refugee's children are uneducated
Due to higher education can't studied

Refugee's camps are filled with many crimes
Because there is no governments and regimes
Especially murder is simple thing in the camp
So every governments try to trouble and tamp

Refugee's camps are built with plastic shelter
Where they can live neither safe nor batter
There is nothing to say about cleanliness
So they cause every disease and sickness

Refugee's camps have very dense crowd
So they have to stay at tent is not broad
Being in the camps, peace is impossible
In the future, own self can't unmanageable

LOST MARTYRDOM

When we have lost our martyrdom
With us, there was none wisdom
We have stayed without peace
So smiles has gone from our face

When we have left our mother land
There was no leader with us to stand
We have been discriminated in our life
That's why in our country happened strife

When we gave up our independence
There was nobody with self confidence
We have felt alone and hardship life
Due to we didn't move as birds are rife

When we have fled from our exile to other
There was no unity between one another
We have lost dignity to leave our country
Because in other nation we have taken entry

HOPE IS HOME

Our hope is to go back home
Which we never think some
Our home land is the best
Which still we could not test

Home is very luxurious place
Where we can live with peace
Home is to be our golden exile
Where we could friendly smile

Going home should try unity
Which has our limitless dignity
Going home should struggle
Which must have much wiggle

Home is located in native land
Where we could proudly stand
Home is the most unforgettable
Where we could feel comfortable

SEA BEACH

Seaside is a pleasing and smooth place
Where tourists come to visit with peace
That is known as a delightful sea beach
Pleasure is absorbed and expressed by each

Beach is a exquisite place with fill of sandy
Where has over floating grey colour cloudy
Sea water is not sweet due to salts contain
From where waves come again and again

Waves is collision then flow over the black rocky
Which is shaped in partial water and below the sky
Seashell is seen not only on stones but also on sand
That is caught and then put in the basket with hand

Shoot the breeze across the sea to the coast fore
Where airplanes fly over the sea and the shore
People sit on sofa seat to take rest with comfort
There are playground to play different types of sport.

A VISIT TO THE ZOO

I visited an amazing place where people excitedly go
There are more than billion types of living things in zoo
I could recognize many living things and their function
Which I never saw with practical soul in my life duration

There are different kind of wild animals normally
Which are encircled in separate room very formally
There are filled with the categories of pet animals
Which are breeded better than other kind of animals

There are many types of fishes swim in pool of water
Where they are kept specially to show to people better
Types of birds are preserved safely into the cage
Where they happily stay and fly together both edge

The group of snakes set in boxes of iron with covering
From where they can't get out and bite without opening
Insects are divided into the groups and protected
From where people are clearly shown and described

BEAUTY OF THE NATURE

Nature is very delightful and beautiful
Where has many things is so wonderful
Appearing the pleasure view in nature
Where including all kinds of creature

Flowing water from both streams and rivers
Fish swims by appearing head in the water
The vision of green emerge due to the tree
Which green leaves slowly move with free

Feeling smell due to the blooming flower
Which dance beautifully by the wind power
South-east breeze blows around the plant
Gentle take oxygen and rest with constant

Birds fly and sing between sky and ground
Clouds float one after one over the mound
Ocean waves come toward sandy shore
Steam evaporates from there more and more

The clearest blue sky changes into twilight
During the sun rises and sets is delight
The moon beautifully shines at night
With the twinkling stars which is bright

THE SUN AND THE STARS

The sun has a face of bright
It rises from east in the morning
The whole day, it gives us sunlight
But it sets to west in the evening

It looks like a electronic bulb
Which gives us light at night
Edison invented that kind of bulb
Which must take sunlight

The stars have a million eyes
When they twinkle bright
The light of the sun dies
While we can know what is called night

Their shape is a type of fish
Which live in the bay
So they are called startfish
The fishermen find them day by day.

<u>**A HEARTFELT GRATITUDE!!**</u>

<u>TO THOSE WHO HAVE READ THIS BOOK</u>

<u>Wishing you well and bright future</u>

www.ingramcontent.com/pod-product-compliance
Lightning Source LLC
Chambersburg PA
CBHW022203160726
48282CB00024B/312
* 9 7 8 9 3 9 5 9 8 3 0 6 8 *